1-2-3 peas

1-2-3 guisantes

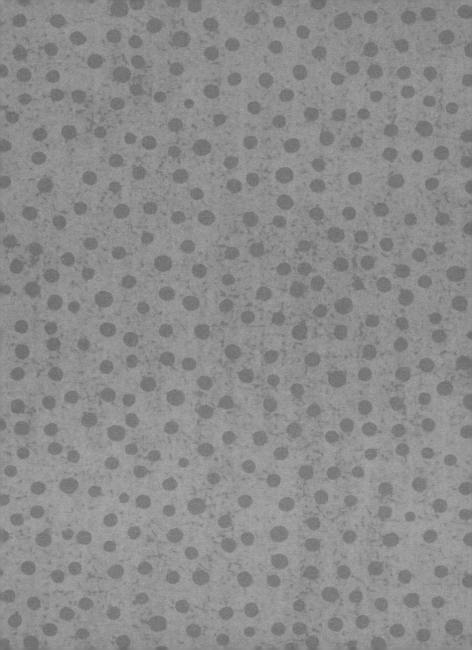

For my mother and father—*love, love, love!*

Para mi mamá y mi papá—*¡los quiero, los quiero, los quiero!*

BEACH LANE BOOKS • An imprint of Simon & Schuster Children's Publishing Division • 1230 Avenue of the Americas, New York, New York 10020 • Copyright © 2012 by Keith Baker • Translation by Argentina Palacios Ziegler • All rights reserved, including the right of reproduction in whole or in part in any form. • BEACH LANE BOOKS is a trademark of Simon & Schuster, Inc. • For information about special discounts for bulk purchases, please contact Simon & Schuster Special Sales at 1-866-506-1949 or business@simonandschuster.com. • The Simon & Schuster Speakers Bureau can bring authors to your live event. For more information or to book an event, contact the Simon & Schuster Speakers Bureau at 1-866-248-3049 or visit our website at www.simonspeakers.com. • Book design by Sonia Chaghatzbanian • The text for this book is set in Frankfurter Medium. • The illustrations for this book are rendered digitally. • Manufactured in the United States of America • 0913 QGL • 10 9 8 7 6 5 4 3 2 1 • Library of Congress Cataloging-in-Publication Data • Baker, Keith, 1953– • 1-2-3 peas / Keith Baker.—1st ed. • p. cm. • One two three peas • 123 peas • Summary: Busy little peas engage in their favorite activities as they introduce the numbers from one to 100. • ISBN 978-1-4424-4551-2 (hardcover) • ISBN 978-1-4424-6575-6 (eBook) • [1. Stories in rhyme. 2. Peas—Fiction. 3. Counting.] I. Title. II. Title: One two three peas. III. Title: 123 peas. • PZ8.3.B175Aah 2012 • [E]—dc23 • 2011034724 • ISBN 978-1-4424-9481-7 (proprietary)

Keith Baker

1-2-3 peas

1-2-3 guisantes

Beach Lane Books New York London Toronto Sydney New Delhi

ONE

pea searching—
look, look, look,

1
UNO
UN
guisante buscando—
a mirar, a mirar, a mirar,

TWO

peas fishing—
hook, hook, hook.

2
DOS
guisantes pescando—
*a enganchar, a enganchar,
a enganchar.*

THReE 3

peas boating—
row, row, row,

**3
TRES**
guisantes navegando—
a remar, a remar, a remar,

FOUR

peas planting—
grow, grow, grow.

4

4
CUATRO
guisantes sembrando—
a crecer, a crecer, a crecer.

FIVE

peas painting—
brush, brush, brush,

5
CINCO
guisantes pintando—
a pintar, a pintar, a pintar,

SIX

peas traveling—
rush, rush, rush.

6
SEIS
guisantes viajando—
a apurarse, a apurarse, a apurarse.

SEVEN

peas jumping—
splash, splash, splash!

7
SIETE
guisantes brincando—
¡a chapotear, a chapotear, a chapotear!

E|GHT

peas racing—*dash, dash, dash.*

8
OCHO
guisantes compitiendo—
a correr, a correr, a correr.

NINE
peas dancing—*round, round, round,*

9
NUEVE
guisantes danzando—
a redondear, a redondear, a redondear,

TEN

peas building—
pound, pound, pound.

10
DIEZ
guisantes construyendo—
a martillear, a martillear, a martillear.

11 12 13 14

15

Eleven to nineteen—*skip, skip, skip!*

1

11 12 13 14 15 16 17 18 19
Once a diecinueve—*ia saltar, a saltar, a saltar!*

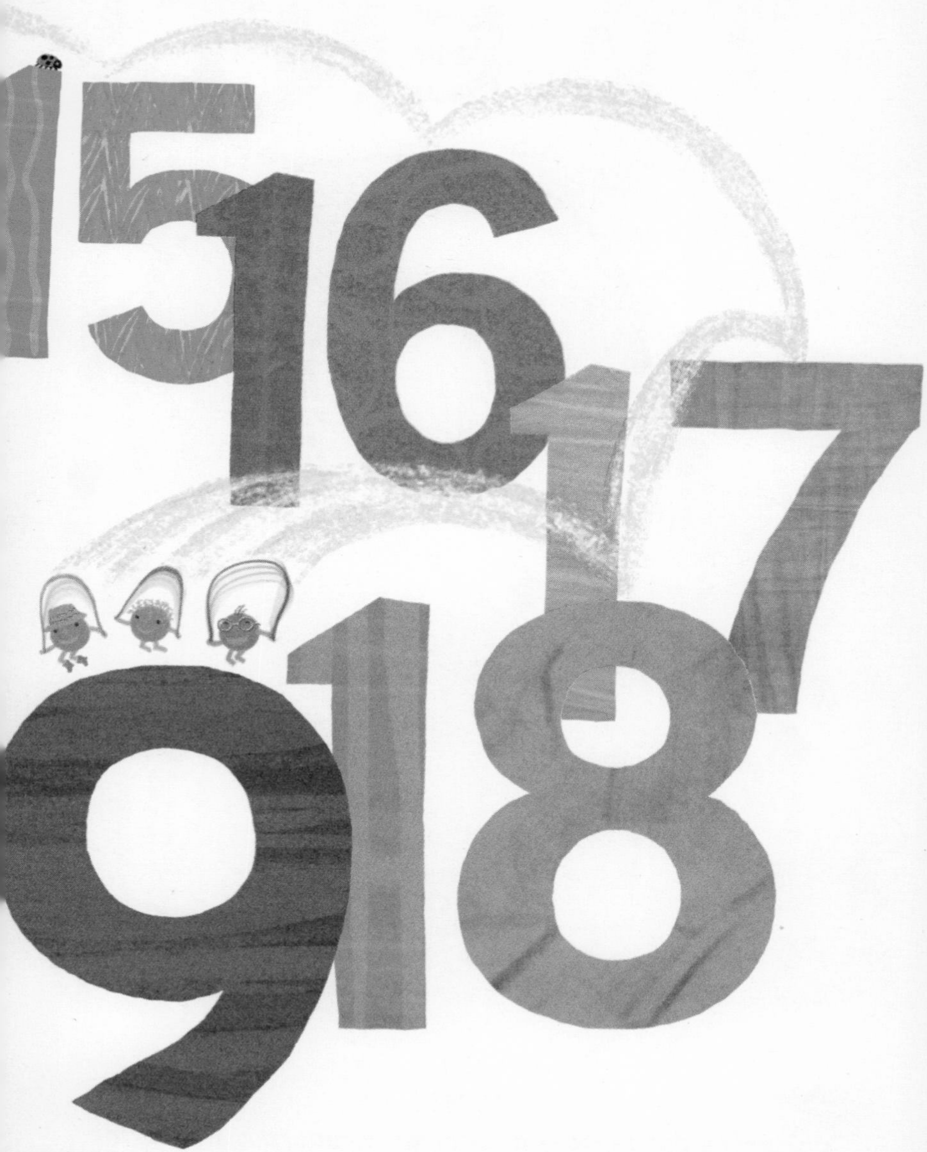
15
16
17
18
9

TWENTY

2

20
VEINTE
guisantes cortando—*a recortar, a recortar, a recortar.*

peas cutting—*snip, snip, snip.*

THIRTY

peas honking—
beep, beep, beep!

30
TREINTA
guisantes bocinando—
¡a pitar, a pitar, a pitar!

FORTY

peas napping—
sleep, sleep, sleep.

40
CUARENTA
guisantes sesteando—
a dormir, a dormir, a dormir.

50
CINCUENTA
guisantes cavilando—
¿cómo, cómo, cómo?

peas puzzling—*how, how, how?*

60
SESENTA
guisantes observando—
¡wow, wow, wow!

SIxTY

peas watching — *wow, wow, wow!*

SEVENTY

peas singing— *la, la, la,*

70
SETENTA
guisantes cantando— *la, la, la,*

EIGHTY peas laughing—ha, ha, ha!

80
OCHENTA
guisantes riéndose—*ija, ja, ja!*

NINET*y*

peas floating—*free, free, free,*

90
NOVENTA
guisantes flotando—*libres, libres, libres,*

peas counting, *hap-pea as can be. . . .*

100
CIEN
guisantes contando—*de lo más felices. . . .*

Please count again with us!

¡Por favor, cuenta otra vez con nosotros!
¿LISTO?
1-2-3 . . .
UNO
DOS
TRES

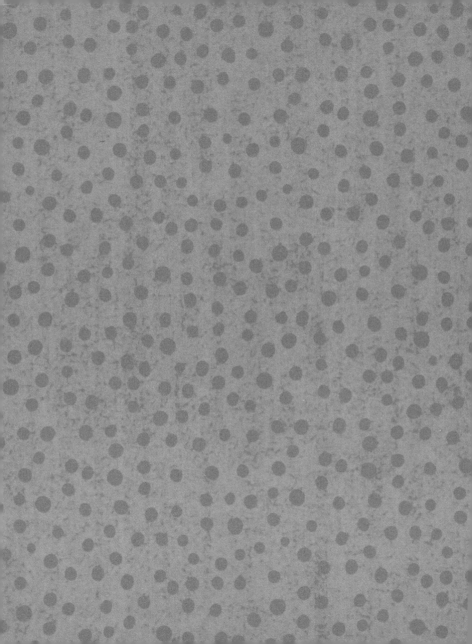

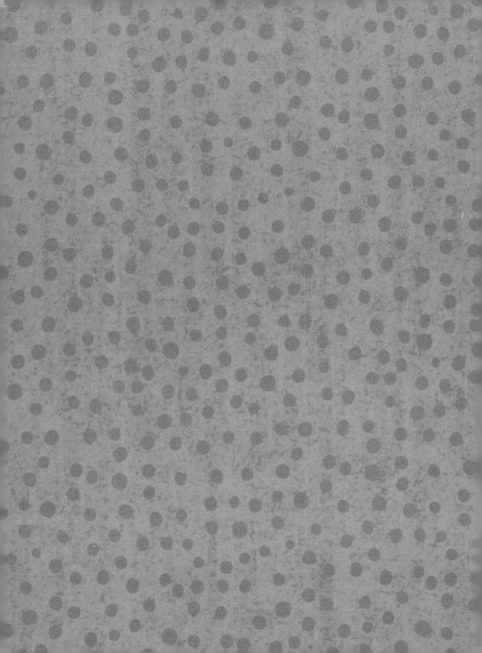